By Suzy Capozzi

Illustrated by Fabio Laguna and Andrea Cagol

 A GOLDEN BOOK · NEW YORK

FROSTY THE SNOWMAN and all related characters and elements © & ™ Warner Bros. Entertainment Inc.
and Classic Media, LLC. Based on the musical composition FROSTY THE SNOWMAN © Warner/Chappell Music, Inc.
(s14)

RHUS32154

Published in the United States by Golden Books, an imprint of Random House Children's Books, a division of Penguin Random House LLC,
1745 Broadway, New York, NY 10019, and in Canada by Penguin Random House Canada Limited, Toronto. Golden Books, A Golden Book,
A Big Golden Book, the G colophon, and the distinctive gold spine are registered trademarks of Penguin Random House LLC.
randomhousekids.com
ISBN 978-0-385-38877-1 (trade)
ISBN 978-0-385-38890-0 (ebook)
MANUFACTURED IN CHINA
20 19 18 17 16 15 14 13

It started with the snow. It was the kind of snow that made happy people happier and giddy people giddier. It even made friends out of enemies. It was the first snow of the season, and it fell on the day before Christmas. When the first snow is also a Christmas snow, something magical is bound to happen.

The children at school wanted to be outside, playing in the snow. Instead, they were in class watching a magician named Professor Hinkle *try* to perform magic tricks.

"Messy! Messy! Messy!" Professor Hinkle grumbled. His magic tricks were not working, so he threw his hat in the trash can. Luckily, his rabbit, Hocus Pocus, rescued it.

Finally, when the school day was over, the
children raced outside. Now they could play
in the snow! They decided to build a snowman.
A little girl named Karen had the most
important job. She would make the
snowman's head.

They gave the snowman a corncob pipe, a button nose, and two eyes made of coal. He looked wonderful! Then it was time to give him a name.

"How about . . . Frosty?" said Karen. All the children cheered and sang a song about him.

Meanwhile, Professor Hinkle was chasing Hocus Pocus.
The rabbit still had his hat. Just when Professor Hinkle
thought he'd finally caught him, the hat flew away on a
gust of winter wind.

Karen caught the hat and put it on Frosty's head. Then something truly extraordinary happened. Frosty the Snowman opened his eyes and said, "Happy birthday!"

"That hat brought Frosty to life!" exclaimed Karen. "It must be magic."

When Professor Hinkle saw how magical his hat was, he snatched it back. With a magical hat, he could become a millionaire magician!

"But we saw Frosty come to life," said Karen.

Professor Hinkle tried to convince Karen and her friends that they were just being silly. "Snowmen can't come to life," he said. But the children knew better.

Hocus Pocus knew better, too. He switched the hat on Professor Hinkle's head with a Christmas wreath. Hocus Pocus hopped with the magical hat to the children and Frosty.

"Look!" cried Karen. "The hat is back!
Let's see if it will bring Frosty back to life again."
Karen placed the hat on Frosty's head.
"Happy birthday!" Frosty exclaimed.

Frosty couldn't believe he could do so many things.

He could make words and MOVE.

He could juggle and almost count to ten. He was even ticklish. He was alive as he could be!

Soon the red in the thermometer started to rise.

"Uh-oh!" exclaimed Frosty. "When the temperature goes up, I start to melt. And when I start to melt, I get all wishy-washy."

Karen realized he needed to go to a place where he'd never melt.

It was decided. The children would put Frosty on a train for the North Pole. They made a party of it. "Let's have a parade!" Frosty exclaimed.

When they finally arrived at the train station, they
realized they didn't have enough money for their tickets.
"No money, no ticket!" shouted the ticket master.
"Now I'll never get to the North Pole," Frosty said.
"Oh, Frosty!" cried Karen. "You just can't melt."

Hocus Pocus pointed Frosty and Karen toward
a little freight train that was just outside the station.
It was heading north and had a refrigerated boxcar.
"What a neat way to travel!" Frosty exclaimed.

Karen joined Frosty on the train. Hocus Pocus hopped aboard, too. There was also one more last-minute traveler: Professor Hinkle. He hid under the train so no one could see him.

A refrigerated boxcar is a splendid way to travel—if you're a snowman or a furry-coated rabbit. But Karen shivered and sneezed.

When the freight train made a brief stop, Frosty quickly got them all off the train.

"Oh, you tricked me!" hollered Professor Hinkle as the train pulled away with him under it. The only thing he could do was jump.

Frosty had to get away from Professor Hinkle—and get Karen someplace warm as quickly as possible. He carried Karen through the woods. She was still sneezing. It was so bitterly cold that even Hocus Pocus, a fur-coated rabbit, started to shiver.

Hocus Pocus got Frosty's attention and pretended
to make a fire.

"Oh, boy, that's one thing I really can't do," said
Frosty. "Guess we'd just better keep moving till we
find someone who can."

Suddenly, they came upon a tiny glen.
The woodland animals were busy decorating
for their big Christmas celebration.

Hocus Pocus spoke to the animals. He explained that Karen needed to warm up by a fire. The animals were delighted to help.

Soon there was a splendid fire crackling away. Karen warmed up quickly by the fire's side. Frosty was careful to stay far away. He didn't want to melt.

Frosty had to get Karen home, but he also needed to get to the North Pole. Suddenly, Hocus Pocus thought of something.

"Santa Claus!" exclaimed Frosty. "That's a great idea!

Hocus Pocus stayed with the woodland animals.
As soon as Santa arrived, he would bring him to
Frosty. Frosty waited patiently. He was close
enough to keep an eye on Karen, but far enough
away from the heat of the fire to keep from melting.

All of a sudden, Professor Hinkle appeared,
startling Karen.

"Give me that hat!" demanded Professor Hinkle.

Frosty raced down the hill to save Karen.

"Get on my shoulders!" said Frosty.

Since he was made of snow, Frosty was the fastest belly-whopper in the world. He and Karen practically flew down the hillside. The professor could hardly keep up.

Luckily for Karen and Frosty, they came upon a greenhouse at the bottom of the hill. Frosty carried Karen inside. He would only stay for a minute, before he melted too much. But Professor Hinkle sneaked up and slammed the door!

"Now I've got you! And the minute you're all melted, the hat will be mine," the magician crowed.

At that very moment, Santa arrived at the
woodland glen. Hocus Pocus explained what
had happened. (Santa spoke fluent Rabbit).
They quickly followed Frosty's path in the snow.

When they arrived at the greenhouse, they saw a terrible sight. Karen was crying beside a puddle. Frosty had melted.

"Christmas snow can never disappear completely," Santa said to Karen gently. "It goes away for a year and it takes the form of spring and summer rain, but you can bet your boots when a jolly December wind kisses it, it will turn into Christmas snow all over again."

Santa opened the door. *Whoosh!* A swirl of magical wind turned the water back into Frosty.

Just as they were about to put the magical hat
on Frosty, Professor Hinkle tried to grab it away.

"If you so much as lay a finger on the brim,
I'll never bring you another Christmas present,"
declared Santa.

Professor Hinkle reluctantly agreed to let Frosty
have the hat.

Once that was all settled, there was only one thing left to do. Santa put the hat on Frosty.

"Happy birthday!" Frosty exclaimed once again. Frosty was alive. Karen was overjoyed. The friends got into Santa's sleigh and took flight.

Santa took Karen home first. Karen was very sad. She didn't want to say goodbye, but she knew Frosty was going to live at the North Pole and could not stay. The two friends hugged and promised to see each other next year.

Every year, Frosty returned with the magical Christmas snow. And every year, there was a celebration—with Frosty leading the parade!

HAPPY HOLIDAYS
and
MERRY CHRISTMAS!